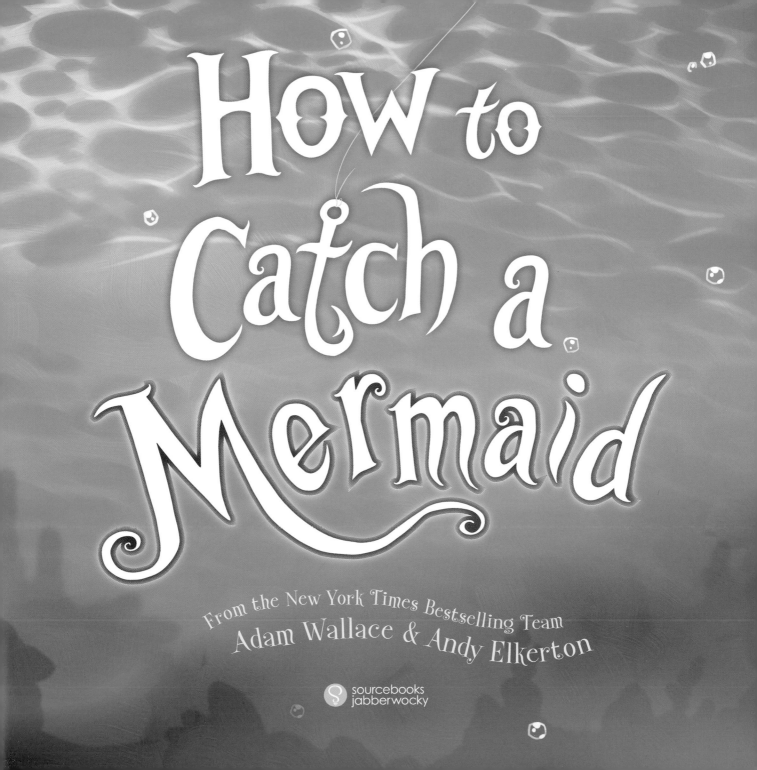

How to Catch a Mermaid

From the New York Times Bestselling Team
Adam Wallace & Andy Elkerton

sourcebooks
jabberwocky

Last week I saw a mermaid.
It's not something I'd pretend!
I'd really like to *Catch* her
so she could be my friend.

We'd have the best adventures.

I'd learn her mermaid ways.

We'd tour her mermaid city.

We'd swim for days and days.

Hey you two, come follow me!
I need you on my TEAM.
The water's where we need to plan
our mermaid-catching scheme.

But *how* to catch a mermaid?
You don't learn this in school.
We'll need to build a gentle trap
and start near the tide pool.

First, I have this **JEWELRY BOX**;
she'll love this bait I bought her.

She can't resist a treasure chest!

Oh, no! It's in the water!

Well mermaids love bright, shiny things;
a CROWN will catch her eye.
We'll lure her in with this new trap
and then our net will fly!

Her seaweed lasso snatched the crown!

We'll need a different plan.

Let's put a sparkly necklace
down inside a giant clam.

She switched the necklace with a **rock** to stop the clam from snapping.

Now she has another prize.

We need some better trapping!

We made a lasso of our own
and hid in the SEAWEED.
She swam too fast for us to catch.
Oh, when will we succeed?

Now let's try to switch it up
and play some **funky beats**.
Maybe that will draw her in?

Oh, no! There's sharks! RETREAT!

We escaped from all the sharks.
That was a **SCARY** scene.
But now we get to up our game
with this cool submarine!

This submarine has robot arms
to catch our fishy lass.
But this mermaid can't be caught.
She really is too *fast!*

It's time to pull out all the stops.

We have to be quite sneaky.

But she heard our trap from far away—

that treasure chest was CREAKY!

Oh, no! Look out! The **SHARKS** are back!

We're doomed—what can we do?

We used up all our traps and bait...

Without some help we're through!

Our mermaid comes to save the day!

She made a trap to save us.

She scares the sharks and scoops us up—
she really is **COURAGEOUS!**

HOORAY! We're safe and back on land.

Three cheers to our mermaid!

We'll miss her smart and clever tricks.

We wish she could have stayed!

Sourcebooks and the colophon are registered trademarks of Sourcebooks, Inc.

The art was first sketched, then painted digitally with brushes designed by the artist.

Published by Sourcebooks Jabberwocky, an imprint of Sourcebooks, Inc.
P.O. Box 4410, Naperville, Illinois 60567-4410
(630) 961-3900
Fax: (630) 961-2168
sourcebooks.com

Library of Congress Cataloging-in-Publication Data is on file with the publisher.

Source of Production: Wing King Tong Paper Products Co. Ltd., Shenzhen, Guangdong Province, China
Date of Production: December 2020
Run Number: 5020653

Printed and bound in China.
WKT 22